W9-AYA-644

FRANKLIN PARK PUBLIC LIBRARY

FRANKLIN PARK, ILL.

Each borrower is held responsible for all library
material drawn on his card and for fines accruing on
the same. No material will be issued until such fine
has been paid.

All injuries to library material beyond reasonable
wear and all losses shall be made good to the
satisfaction of the Librarian.

Replacement costs will be
billed after 42 days overdue.

I am Paulo Marcelo Feliciano,
and soon I will shine like a star.
I will light up the homes in this favela.
I will light every home in Brazil.

Like Garrincha, Pelé, and Ronaldo,
who have all played in these alleys,
I will play my way to stardom,
because I'm a champion, too.

Soccer Star

Mina Javaherbin   illustrated by Renato Alarcão

AUTHOR'S NOTE

In Brazil, some children work hard for a living to overcome a stubborn opponent: poverty. This experience of life's hardship, being engaged in the survival arena from childhood, has helped shape Brazil's solid team of stars shining atop the world of soccer. My story is an homage to all soccer stars who have risen and continue to rise up from poverty.

To Mom and Dad
M. J.

To the Brazilian kids who once dreamed of becoming soccer stars
R. A.

CANDLEWICK PRESS

Text copyright © 2014 by Mina Javaherbin. Illustrations copyright © 2014 by Renato Alarcão. All rights reserved. No part of this book may be reproduced, transmitted, or stored in an information retrieval system in any form or by any means, graphic, electronic, or mechanical, including photocopying, taping, and recording, without prior written permission from the publisher. First edition 2014. Library of Congress Catalog Card Number 2013944008. ISBN 978-0-7636-6056-7. This book was typeset in ITC Fenice. The illustrations were done in sepia ink with color added digitally. Candlewick Press, 99 Dover Street, Somerville, Massachusetts 02144. visit us at www.candlewick.com. Printed in Dongguan, Guangdong, China. 14 15 16 17 18 19 TLF 10 9 8 7 6 5 4 3 2 1

E
430-5218

FRANKLIN PARK PUBLIC LIBRARY
Franklin Park, Illinois

I am Paulo Marcelo Feliciano,
and when I'm a soccer star,
my mother won't have to work long hours
and I won't have to miss her so much.

All day, I help Senhor da Silva fish.
After work, I practice soccer with him.

At night my sister, Maria, and I
read and write and play.
I teach her soccer moves;

she teaches me math from school.

This morning, Mamãe left me enough *pão de queijo*
to share with my soccer team.
We'll need the energy tonight.
We have a big game on the beach!

I swallow my cheese buns and pack some for Maria.
We run out the door to her school.

And we dribble past our neighborhood.

I kick the ball to Maria.
She heads it back to me.

I pass the ball to Maria again,
and this time she knees it up.

I kick it past her little shoulders.
She fires her bicycle kick!

Maria sees that I'm impressed.
"So *now* can I be on your team?"

She asks me this day after day.
But my answer is always the same:
"Our team's rule is *no girls*."

Maria looks sad, so I say,
"We'll practice more after my game, OK?"
She smiles a little, waves good-bye,
and walks to her class.

I dribble to Carlos, who's shining shoes
with his sisters by his side.
I know that one day, his fancy footwork
will score us brilliant goals.

I leave a bun for my goalie, Jose.
He is diving for tourists this morning.
I know that one day, he will dive for the ball
and take our team to the top.

I dribble to Givo, who helps the dancers
and works on the carnival floats.
I know that one day, he will dance with the ball
and the fans will cheer his moves.

I dribble to Pedro, at the coconut grove.
He is climbing up a tree.
I know that one day, he'll climb to glory
and harvest us fortune and trophies.

I am Paulo Marcelo Feliciano.
I will lead my team to the top,
and the crowd will cheer my soccer name:

"Captain Felino! The star!"

"Felino! Hurry! You're late!" Senhor da Silva shouts.

We're off to the ocean, and when it's time,
I cast my net in the deep.
Wild storm clouds
appear fast
in the sky above.

Over and over, I cast the net.
I gather and pull in the catch.
Senhor da Silva and I discuss
my game plans for tonight.
I keep an eye on the horizon
and hope that the clouds disappear.

Senhor da Silva finally says, "Felino,
enough for today."
The gray clouds suddenly sail away—
  away from the beach,
  away from my game.

We steer the boat to the shore,
and my team gathers to help.

We plan and practice our game.

Jose will fly,

Givo will bounce,

Carlos will kick,

Pedro will shoot,

and Felino will score!

Maria arrives, along with two of Carlos's sisters, and so does the other team.

My sister runs to my teammates and asks,
"Please can I play on your team?"
"She's really good!" I say with a grin,
and Carlos's sisters cheer.
But the boys cross their arms, say no, and frown.
"Not this time," I say to Maria.

The game starts.
Their forward attacks.

Jose jumps up and — *whoosh!*

He lands on his wrist.
I run over to him.
"The wrist isn't broken," Senhor da Silva says,
"but I think Jose should rest."

Givo stands in as goalie,
and we're short a player.

"Maria?" I ask my team.
Givo votes no,
Pedro votes yes,
and Carlos is fine either way.

It's up to me,
and my vote is for change.
I wave to my sister and say, "It's time!"
and Maria runs onto the field.

Maria runs all over the field.
She heads to Pedro,
she knees to Carlos,
and when the ball flies
past her little shoulders,
she fires her bicycle kick

and she scores!

I am Paulo Marcelo Feliciano,
the captain of this team.
No storm, fall, or useless old rule
can keep us from a win.

Our fans will one day call us the stars.
We will light every home in Brazil.